Redemption OF THE Lost

THE HAUNTED CITY II

WORKS BY TY'RON W. C. ROBINSON II

BOOKS

DARK TITAN UNIVERSE SAGA

MAIN SERIES
Dark Titan Knights
The Resistance Protocol
Tales of the Scattered
Tales of the Numinous
Day of Octagon
Crossbreed
Heaven's Called

Forthcoming
The Resistance/Protectors War
Underworld
Magicks and Mysticism

SPIN-OFFS
In A Glass of Dawn: The Casebook of Travis Vail
Maveth: Bloodsport

Forthcoming
The Curse of The Mutant-Thing
Trail of Vengeance
War of The Thunder Gods

THE HAUNTED CITY SAGA
The Legendary Warslinger: The Haunted City I
Battle of Astolat: A Haunted City Prequel (KOBO Exclusive)
Redemption of the Lost: The Haunted City II
Consequences of the Suffering: The Haunted City III (Forthcoming)

SYMBOLUM VENATORES
Symbolum Venatores: The Gabriel Kane Collection
Hod: A Symbolum Venatores Book
Symbolum Venatores: War of The Two Kingdoms (Forthoming)

OTHER BOOKS
Lost in Shadows: A Novel
Lost in Shadows: Remastered
Accounts of The Dead Days
The Book of The Elect
Hallow Sword: Cursed(KOBO Exclusive)
Dark Titan Omnibus: Volume 1
The Extended Age Omnibus
Frightened!: The Beginning
EverWar Universe: Knights & Lords (Forthcoming)
Dark Titan Omnibus: Volume 2 (Forthcoming)

REDEMPTION OF THE LOST

THE HAUNTED CITY II

TY'RON W. C. ROBINSON II

CONTENTS

EXODUS

MYSTERIOUS WAYS

I

Moving on across the Western World, leaving the mystical mountains, the Warslinger led his new allies into the deeper parts of the revelations. Moving on from their previous encounters with foes and otherworldly scenarios. Calm and collective. More of a unit. Cody and Beth have agreed to align themselves with the Warslinger on his quest to reach The Haunted City. After seeing a glimpse of the fabled location atop the mountain. The mountain is now known as the Mount of Divination.

While they walked down the straightened path, which they knew was a road due to the tire tracks and horse prints in the dirt. Cody could see something in the horizon further out. Objects near reaching the clouds. He pointed it toward them.

"Sir, what are those?"

Henrich glanced up and saw the objects in the sky. From his eyesight, they appeared as sharp needles standing above the ground, almost touching the first heaven. Beth took a step forward, shading her eyes from the sun with her hand.

"Are those buildings?"

"Yes." Henrich said. "They are."

"What place is further down?" Cody wondered. "Is that where we're heading next?"

"If it's in our path, then yes. If not, we continue moving on."

After miles of walking, they came to a stop. Taking a moment to relax and rest, Henrich turned to his right and saw the city closer. He could see the buildings which stood tall. Cody glanced at them, looking at their height.

"I've never seen such structures before."

"Seriously?" Beth said. "You've never seen skyscrapers"

"No. What are these skyscrapers?"

"They're buildings, boy." Henrich said. "Just buildings. Although, they're not called skyscrapers anymore. Hell, they haven't been called that in almost four hundred years."

"What do they call them now?"

"Breachers of the Heavens in the Western World. Domebreakers in the Eastern World."

They continued their move toward the city ahead. Very familiar, yet old. Old due to the amount of years which have gone by since its inception. Henrich was there when the city was founded as he stood there now at its end. Or so it may seem to be. Finally, their walk had ceased as they stood in the entrance to the city.

"What was the name of this place?" Cody asked.

"Now, Old Los Angeles." Henrich declared. "A place once called a city of angels. Now, it's a resting place for the lost, the weary, and mostly, the wicked."

II

Walking through the dirty and trash-filled street of Old Los Angeles, the city has become a rest stop and a salvage point for nearby everyone who can survive the time within. Building have crumbled into rubble. Others stand tall as their once attractive appearance has faded into a plain dusty tower.

"What is that stench?" Cody looked around, covering his face.

"It's the river." Henrich replied. "It's dead."

"What's happened here." Beth wondered, looking at the city's destruction. She continued looking and saw cracks throughout the ground of the city.

"What are all these cracks?"

'A great *worldquake* came through here during the time of the War of the West." Henrich stated. "Destroyed much of whatever was in its way. People evacuated without notice. Many died. Few managed to survive and fled to the nearest region."

"And what of the rest of this place?" Cody asked. "The buildings and such?"

"Time." Henrich said. "The movement of time has transformed this place into what it's become. During my youth, this city was a prosperous place. Yet, that was all before the War of the West."

"Where I'm from, Los Angeles thrives. It's a big city. Resembles this one, but fully functioning."

"Must be pleasant." Henrich said.

"I wouldn't call it pleasant. But, it's lively."

"How many wars have there been?"

"Too many to count. I was in most of them."

"You fought in the Shooter War?" Cody asked.

"I was a front liner in that war. Very young. Eager to do the killing when it was necessary."

"And what are you now?" Beth wondered. "Are you still that same young man or are you more mature?"

Henrich sighed and shrugged.

"Little bit of both I presume."

Upon walking, Henrich caught the wind of several men scattered through the area. Five of them, dressed in ragged clothing. Torn pants and worn-out boots. They smelled of the old city. The stench of oil and must covered the area. Henrich slowly moved his hands toward his shooters. Landon spotted the hand motions and signaled toward Beth as the men inched closer.

"Well, what do we have here." One man gestured. "A couple of stranders."

"We're just passing through." Henrich said. "We desire no trouble."

"Sorry to hear your plea, good sir." Another man said, approaching Henrich. "But, you're in our city and here, we make the rules."

"And what rules to you imply to stranders?"

"We take what they have and, usually, kill them. Very simple."

Henrich nodded, looking at the men surrounded. Landon gave Henrich a nod and so did Beth. Henrich nodded back before turning toward the man in front of him.

"Now, what do you three have to offer? Water, food, herbs?"

"Perhaps, they can lend us the young woman." One man spoke from the distance. "We haven't had a new woman come through these lands in months."

"That will not happen." Beth said.

"Oh, she speaks."

"Don't take her lightly." Henrich said. "Don't take any of us as such."

"Nobody's taking anyone lightly. Just give us something of yours and you can pass."

"Not giving any of you anything. Except for one word of advice."

"A word of advice?" the man shrugged. "What advice?"

"You reap what you sow."

"I wh-"

Before the man could finish, Henrich fired a shot at the man's head. Landon and Beth turned to the men behind them and fired shots of their own. Henrich turned toward the others and let out blasts, killing the small gang. After the shotfire, silence stilled the air.

"This was on them." Henrich proclaimed. "Not us."

The three continued on their journey as the vultures appeared from the air and covered the bodies of the dead men.

III

Walking further through the city, something caught Henrich and he grabbed quickly to what it is. He moved with more speed; a vigilant look covered his face. There was no expression. Only focus. Cody and Beth paced themselves to keep up with the Warslinger.

"Sir, what is it?" Landon asked. "Why are you moving at this pace?"

'There's something here. Something in the city."

"Like what?" Beth wondered. "A portal out of here?"

"No." Henrich stated. "Something more. I haven't sensed it since the Battle of Astolat."

"Astolat?" Landon said. "It's fine and well."

"Now it is."

"I don't know what either of you are speaking of. But, what is Astolat."

"A place." Henrich said. "A tale for another time."

The Three made their move through the city. Not one stop was made nor was a break. They each moved with focus and speed. Unified in their mission to find whatever it is which has caught the attention of the Warslinger. They passed by more gangs, prostitutes, beaten-down shelters which stood empty, apart from a few homeless remaining in its shadows.

Still moving, a man indivertibly bumped into Henrich. He neither flinched nor hid himself. He stood bold, just as the Three. However, his focus was on the Warslinger and it was unsettling to Cody and Beth. Henrich has been through these situations' countless times. It was nothing to him.

"Pardon me, sir." The man said, raising his head.

"Your eyes." Cody said.

The man was elderly and blind. He stood before them, dressed in what would assume rags and a coat. His unkempt hair flowed with the sudden gusts of the air. Henrich stared at the man and the man did the same to the Warslinger.

"Your essence." The man said of Henrich. "It is familiar. Ancient-like."

"And you can tell from?"

"On your sides, the shooters. Their power can be felt."

"Wait, you can sense the shooters?" Landon said. "How's that possible?"

"Appears this man has seen many things in his life." Henrich said. "Tell me, sir, how you've come to learn of a Warslinger's arkshooters?"

"I used to travel a lot in my prime years. I've seen the wonders of the Eastern World. The structures of Old Egypt and the Temple of Old Jerusalem. I lived in Old London before it became New London. I'm sure you're understanding my words well."

"I am" Henrich said. "But, we're not here to hear stories. We're tracking something down and it is of great importance we discover the source."

"You sense it as well." The man said with a smile. "Good. I am not the only one."

"Do you know what it may be?"

"I have a clue. I am not sure it is direct."

"How about this. Where were you when you felt it as its strongest?"

"Almost out of the downtown area. Near the outside

points of the city."

Henrich nodded.

"Great." Cody said. "Let's get a move on."

"As we should." Henrich said. "Thank you for your aid, elder."

The elderly man bowed before Henrich. His hands and face flat on the concrete grounds. Cody and Beth stood still, confused. Henrich kneeled and help the man to his feet. The man seemed to have been crying as he was on the ground. Not of sorrow or sadness, but of hope.

"Why bow before me?" Henrich wondered.

"It has been a long time since I've encountered a servant of El. Forgive me if my behavior was out of place."

"No need. Only do not bow before me or any other Warslinger. We're just servants as you said. If you choose to worship El, worship him in spirit and in truth."

The man nodded as the Three went their way.

IV

Walking along their projected path, tracking the source of the aura, Henrich started to notice their sudden exit of the downtown region. Due to the fact of staring at a deserted road ahead. In the distance, there were no tall buildings. Skyscrapers only stood behind them. Quiet and motionless. They could only see fields of half-dead grass and withered trees. A combination of light sand and soil covered the ground.

"Where does this road lead?" Cody wondered.

"We'll have to find out." Henrich replied. "The source is coming from along this path."

"I have to ask, what is this source?" Beth questioned. "Is it some kind of paranormal thing or something larger?"

"Where you're from, they would call it a paranormal occurrence. Here, it's a spiritual matter. One of a dire need."

"How dire are you talking?"

"A serious matter." Henrich professed. "Plus, it reminds me of things I've felt in my youth. Training and growing in this life. Sources like this were always around. A constant hesitation to all who served the benevolency of the universe."

"You know, you're going to have to tell me more about your world." Beth gestured. "It's very, mystique compared to where I'm from. Yet, very similar in a lot of ways. Almost as if this world is my world's future or vice versa."

Henrich turned to Beth. A sudden urge to speak something in his mind. He looked down at the sandy soil and back up toward Cody and Beth.

"Better you wait for the day to come and be prepared, rather than the day comes and you're not ready. Besides, this could all be a test for you. Or a purpose."

"What purpose is it for someone or something to take me from my home?"

"A higher purpose. For good or for evil. Only you'll know when the test is complete."

"And you know this how?"

"I've seen many like you before. Mindset-wise. Never have I ever encountered someone from a world you've spoken about. A place where there's paranormal investigators and go looking for trouble with the malevolency."

"There's a lot of things the people should know about the world they live in."

"And yet, how many of them disagree with that statement?" Henrich asked. "Many. Only a few can manage this knowledge. Seeing as how you've not gone crazy proves you're one of the few."

Beth nodded with respect. A calmness came over her.

"I appreciate that."

"I'm only being honest." Henrich replied. "Come on, we need to keep moving."

They continued their journey, following the aura. Ironically, Cody and Beth could not see what the Warslinger was keeping his focus on. A strange, violet trail of mist covered the air above them. His eyes were focused on it and marked it for an easy track to the source.

V

The deserted road is well, deserted. No sign of life seemed to be around the area as Henrich tracked the source. The surrounding areas were still. Not a sound nor a chirp of a bird, nor a bark of a dog, a screech of a cat. Nothing. Only complete quietness except for the wind bristling against the trees and grass.

"The breeze is nice." Beth said.

"It's to keep us cooled down." Henrich said. "Felt the same breeze when I was in the desert on this journey."

"I'm just curious as to where they come from." Cody said. "Like where a breeze starts and where does it end?"

"A question for another time, eh." Henrich grinned.

After walking several miles, not distant from downtown Old Los Angeles, they come across a sign. The sign detailed a location covered with people and life. Written in *Old Tongue*, yet Beth approached the sign.

"You can read that?" Cody asked.

"Yeah. It's English."

"It's what?" Cody said.

"One of the past languages of this World." Henrich professed. "I can read it as well."

"Wow. You have to teach me."

"I will." Henrich said.

Beth read the sign. She looked ahead, her eyes on the

deserted road and what's ahead.

"The sign says there's a church down this path."

"Might explain the source." Henrich said. "then, we'll go there. See what's ongoing."

"Didn't that mirror warn you of some kind of church." Cody referenced. "It all sounds familiar."

"That's why we must go. To confirm the mirror's prophetic words."

"I understand. I guess."

They passed the sign and continued further, seeking to reach the church of the sign.

FINDING THE CHURCH

I

Following the trail and the aura source above, the surroundings increasing with trees. While they walk, Henrich showed a peculiar expression, taking notice of the area. It seemed to appear somewhat familiar to his memory.

"What is it, sir?" Cody asked.

"This place. This area, it's appearing familiar to me. I've been here before. Long ago."

"Then, you know where we're headed." Beth said.

"We're reaching the San Fernando Valley."

"The Valley?" Beth said. "It's still a dwelling place in this World?"

"Not sure. But, this trail and the source are coming from that direction."

As they walked, a bright flash of light appeared before them. Nearly blinding them of the path. Henrich raised his arm to avoid the light and just as quickly as it appeared it vanished. They each looked and saw someone standing before them. A young man. Wearing the clothes of a vagabond with a weathered fedora the colors of dried bark.

Cody and Beth were unaware as to who the young man could be. Henrich, however kept his gaze keen.

"I've heard of you." Henrich said. "The Jumper."

"That's what they call me nowadays? Man, I would've preferred something more creative."

"Who are you?" Cody asked.

"Pardon my manners, I am the Kroger Kid."

"Kroger Kid?" Beth said. "Like from a grocery store?"

"What?" The Kroger Kid gestured. "No, I travel between worlds."

"Really." Cody said.

"He travels across the Four Worlds." Henrich added. "It's how he gets from place to place within seconds."

"Hold on, Warslinger. I can also travel to worlds outside of the Four."

"Then, let me ask this question. Have you traveled to the Outer-World? Have you seen the City?"

"Have I? It's a place of great spiritual power. But, it isn't designed for me."

"How come?" Beth wondered. "I'm sure there's a reason."

"I'm the kind of guy who does things on his own terms."

"Why bother us to begin with?" Henrich asked.

"Because I heard about a Warslinger who went through the towns of Savel and Hevoc. I noticed the Cailleach was no longer doing her little tests near the Valley of Death. Those dirty Scavengers are all dead and the Mercenary Man's body was found in another dimension."

"You've seen all of this?"

"I might have been hiding behind corners and suchlike. Maybe."

Henrich shook his head. "Why are you here now?"

"Because I know what you're seeking and where you're heading. That source does take you somewhere. But, it's best you do not do what you did to Savel or Hevoc."

"I had no choice."

"We all have choices, Warslinger."

"And yours is to stop my journey to reaching the City?"

"Why yes." The Kroger Kid giggled. "I can't let you pass."

"I wasn't asking for a pass."

Henrich pulled out his shooter without hesitation and fired. The Kroger Kid illuminated himself, vanishing in a blast of light. The three looked around and unnoticeably, the Kroger Kid returned behind them,

"I have to lure you away in one shape or another!" The Kroger Kid yelled with excitement.

Henrich looked to his left and spotted his other shooter was gone. He stared at the Kroger Kid, who was waving his shooter in the air after snatching it from Henrich's side. The Kid took off into the woods, laughing maniacally.

"Seriously." Beth said.

"He took your shooter, sir." Cody said. "What are we going to do?"

"Get it back." Henrich replied as he ran after the Kroger Kid into the wilderness.

"Ah, man." Cody said, following the Warslinger and Beth.

Henrich ran through the forest after the Kroger Kid, who would appear and reappear in certain locations. Cody and Beth followed fast on their feet. Henrich fired a shot every time the Kroger Kid appeared. While he continued to vanish with a quick flash of light, Henrich moved faster with every step. Shooter firing. Cody did the same as did Beth.

"I've never seen him move that fast." Cody mentioned.

"He wants his gun back." Beth replied. "What would do think he'll be doing?"

"Wait. Gun? You mean his shooter."

"Yes, that's what I mean."

The Warslinger continued firing shots at the appearing Kroger Kid, who proceeded to mock him as they moved through the trees.

"It might take you all night to catch up!" The Kroger Kid yelled.

"You're a nuisance!" Henrich said. "A pain!"

"I've heard worse!"

The Kid vanished once more and appeared before Cody, tripping him onto the ground and teleporting behind Beth, shoving her against the nearby tree. The Kid vanished with only a laugh echoing through the forest. Henrich caught up to the two, helping them up.

"He tripped me." Cody said.

"You'll be fine." Henrich replied. "Beth, how are you?"

"Just a scratch. It's nothing."

While they spoke, the Kid appeared above them, sitting

in the tree. Giggling.

"Here's the thing, stranders." The Kid said, getting their attention.

"Not again." Henrich said, raising up his shooter and firing.

The Kid snatched the bullet from the air and returned it to Henrich's shooter. Right in the chamber.

"Did he just give you the bullet back?" Cody said. "And put it back in the shooter?"

"I have skills, my boy!" The Kid said.

"Give me back my other shooter and let us on our way."

"I'm sorry, Warslinger. As much as I respect you and your kind, I cannot let you bother the World beyond this forest. For the Valley has seen better days since their union."

"What union?" Henrich wondered. "Who's waiting on the other end of this forest? Who's dwelling in the ruins of the Valley?"

"Ah, now that is a conversation for another time."

The Kid raised his right index finger and Henrich's shooter was returned to his side. Henrich looked and grabbed it, holding now both shooters aimed at the Kid. Cody held the blast shooter and Beth grabbed the machete from Henrich's coat. The Kid applauded the team.

"Looks like a new Heptad is resurging from my point of view."

"You will let us pass." Henrich proclaimed. "Or else, you'll wish you could teleport to a place of peace permanently."

"More threats." The Kid laughed. "As long as you're in this region, near the Valley, I will not cease to stop you."

The Kid gazed up toward the afternoon sky, seeing the sun. He pointed toward the sky.

"Appears the sun will be going down soon, you're in this forest, and I will not let you pass. Therefore, you have two options before you. Return to where you came from or spend the night in these woods and wish for a better morrow.”

Henrich stared at the Kid with intensity. Cody and Beth remained still. The Kid didn’t take his eyes off the Warslinger and neither did he. Henrich took the shot with both shooters and the Kid disappeared once more. Henrich placed the shooters to his side, turning to Cody and Beth.

“Looks like we’re camping here for the night.”

Later in the night, after setting up camp with the equipment they carried in Henrich’s bag, the three sat together under the dark sky and stars above. The silence of the wilderness and the still wind. A fire was kindled for heat as the surroundings gravely dropped.

“This world is strange.” Beth said. “Very.”

“So, it doesn’t get cold where you’re from?” Cody asked.

“It does. But, not on a day like this. It’s usually warm. Somewhat cool.”

“Your world isn’t that different from ours.” Henrich said.

“Then, let me in on it. Tell me about this place. Your Worlds.”

Henrich nodded and drew closer toward the flame. Holding his hands over the fire.

“At the beginning of time, our sense of time, the Master known as El created everything from our world to yours and others beyond. Here, He created *Adamah* and it combines the Four Worlds. Afterwards, he created the stars, the heavens and the five seas. Four surround the Four Worlds and one sits in the center of them all; *Tsaphon* is the sea of the north, *Teman* is the sea of the south, *Qedem* is the sea of the east, and *Maarab* is the sea of the west. Together, they form *Tehomayim*, the great sea of the Worlds. The center sea is called the *Sea of Tabbur*, which signifies the connection of the Four Worlds. The Worlds themselves are as follows; *Yaphean*, the Northern World. A place of sheer winter and diverse kingdoms. From Anchor Bay to Old Camelot and what is now New London. Then, He created *Khamain*, the Southern World. A land filled with kingdoms and lush landscapes. The home of Old Egypt and the Amazon City. A place of beauty. Next was *Shemia*, the Eastern World. The land where El placed His name. The home of Old Jerusalem, my home and Mount Sinai. The land which is the birthplace of the Warslingers of the Heptad."

"I didn't know you were from Old Jerusalem." Cody said. "You've seen its fall."

"I was there when it fell. The moment where we lost. The defeat of the Heptad. The end of the Warslingers. Betrayal and unjust ones claimed the land soon after. That day was named the Fall of Old Jerusalem."

"And what of the other World?" Beth asked. "The Western one?"

"You speak of *Arzareth*, the Western World. Which we are currently placed. The land where the Warslingers were dispersed. A place of prophecy. Yet, there is one more world. The realm where the spirits dwell and judgment is set. The realm where The Haunted City itself sits amongst the Gate of the City and the Kingdom of Order. That place is called *Ruachayim*, the Outer-World."

"Then, what happened next?" Cody asked curiously.

"After the Worlds were formed, to keep the seas from overtaking them, El created a boundary made of steel-like ice and called the place *Qeramah*. Then, before Man walked upon the worlds, the animals were formed. Yet, there were also those above. The Sons of El, a group of spiritual beings. We know them as the Seraph."

"You mean like angels." Beth said.

"Yes. One deemed himself worthy of ruler ship. A war broke out in the Outer-World and he was defeated. Upon his downfall, his essence and dark spirit spread throughout the Four Worlds and the Malevolency was born, eventually consuming the generations of Man which came after. An opposition to El's Benevolency. That is why the Warslingers of the Heptad were created. To combat the forces made from the spread of the Malevolency."

"So, you've seen a lot during your years." Beth said. "Which brings me to a question. How old are you?"

"How old you do perceive me to be?"

"You look as if you're in your mid-forties. Perhaps early forties."

"There's no way he's in his forties." Cody said. "Impossible."

"What do you mean? He looks forty to me."

"Because I'm in my mid-twenties."

"No, you're not." Beth said. "You're at least sixteen. Maybe seventeen."

"He's in his twenties." Henrich said. "I'm certain."

"I don't understand. People in my world look much older in their mid-twenties. Then, how old are you if you're not in your forties?"

"I've been around for over five hundred years." Henrich said. "Humans age much slower in the Four Worlds than yours I'm assuming?"

"Very much so."

Henrich looked up, still seeing the aura trail in the air glowing in the night hour. He also sensed the magic of the Kroger Kid lurking around the trees.

"Best we get some sleep."

"What of that Kid?" Beth wondered.

"We'll deal with him in the morning."

The Warslinger put out the fire and sleep fell upon the three.

III

They awoke right at the brink of dawn. Henrich stood tall, gazing toward the morning sky and looking around the trees for the Kroger Kid. Beth and Cody rose up from their slumber, seeing Henrich gazing around the area.

'What is it?"

"Seeing if he's around." Henrich said. "He's watching us. I'm sure of it."

"Well, he can't possibly keep us in this forest for long." Cody added. "I mean, what's the worse he could do to us?"

While talking, the sound of a breaking branch echoed through the forest. Henrich caught the sound quickly while Cody and Beth talked. Henrich approached them, waving his hand.

"Something's out here." Henrich said steadily.

The Warslinger reached and raised up his shooter. He looked around and the sound increased. Moving closer. Cody and Beth stood up, holding weapons of their own. Henrich turned back around, following the sound and could see what it was. It was approaching them fast.

"There it is." Henrich said.

"There's what?" Cody asked, turning around to see what Henrich saw. "Oh no."

"What is it?" Beth asked.

They found themselves staring at three scorpions. Larger than Beth had ever seen. A dark brown with a hint of gold in their shelled bodies. Their eyes burning violet and the tips of their tails sharp as blades. Henrich and Cody took steps forward with their shooters. The scorpions hissed with fury and their tails slammed against the ground, tossing dirt and leaves into the air.

"What are those?!" Beth asked.

"Dire Scorpions." Henrich said.

"Like the wolves?!"

"Yes."

Henrich fired several shots toward the scorpions, but their hollow hide was too dense for the bullets to penetrate. Cody turned to Beth with haste, dropping his weapon.

"Hand me the blastshooter!"

Beth tossed him the shooter and he fired a round toward the first scorpion. The blastshooter proved effective as it burst the shell on the top of the scorpion. The shell slid off with pus. Cody fired rounds toward the other two, blowing one's claw and the other's tail off. The scorpions screeched with agony.

"What's next?" Cody asked. "We keep shooting?"

"We'll have to get closer." Henrich said.

Henrich pulled out his machete and ran toward the first scorpion. He jumped up as the claws reached out to snatch him. Henrich raised the machete and impaled it into the creature, killing it with the blow. The scorpion fell to the ground as the other two ambushed Henrich. Cody ran after him and fired another round from the blastshooter into the scorpion's face, blowing it off as it slid from the body. Henrich grabbed the remaining one's tail and used it to impale the scorpion itself. The Warslinger stepped back as the scorpion fell dead by its own tail.

"That's it." Cody said. "We won."

"It seems." Henrich replied.

"Are those things native to this place?" Beth asked, looking at the bodies in awe.

"Dire Scorpions don't belong here. They're mostly found in the Eastern World. In Old Egypt."

"Then, how did you three end up here?" Cody asked.

"The Kroger Kid." Henrich replied. "He brought them here. To distract us. To cause us to stumble from our mission."

"You're telling me there's more of these and other creatures as big as this?" Beth asked.

"A lot more." Henrich said. "You would be amazed at the creatures within the Four Worlds."

Cody looked around the trees and approached Henrich.

"Do you think he's watching?"

"I know he is."

Henrich stepped forward and looked around.

"Kroger Kid!" Henrich yelled. "I know you're watching us, and you saw what we did and what we're capable of. Either you return to me my shooter and let us pass. Or, you will suffer the same fate, if not worse like your pets from Shemia!"

The burst of light reappeared in the trees above them, Henrich looked, spotting the Kroger Kid moving through them as if he was running on air. Henrich pressed forward, grabbing his gear and ran after the Kid. Cody and Beth followed.

IV

Chasing the Kroger Kid through the forest, the eyes of the Warslinger were locked onto the young man. The Kid raised his hands and threw energy balls of light toward the three, stumbling them from the chase. No matter, Henrich proceeded past the light, for his eyes were not shaken nor blinded by the brightness. Beth had to pause, and Cody stumbled in his running, nearly tripping himself.

"We need to keep up!" Henrich yelled.

The Kid threw more energy balls and once they were in the air, Henrich raised up his shooter, firing rounds into the balls, causing them to explode and spreading the brightness of the light.

"That's not possible." The Kid said to himself, still running and teleporting.

"I can hear you." Henrich responded. "This game of yours is over."

The Kid moved and vanished into a tree in the midst of the forest. This tree was larger, thicker in size. The branches were nearly long as the tress standing around them. Cody and Beth caught up to the Warslinger, staring in awe at the massive tree.

"What is this?" Cody wondered.

"The Kid went inside the tree." Henrich said. "He's not leaving."

"How can you be sure?" Beth asked. "I mean he did show us he can teleport."

"Because this tree is his home. He dwells in it."

"I don't understand."

"The outer layer appears as a mammoth tree. But, the interior, is like a home. A mansion for his kind."

Henrich kicked the tree, causing it to rattle. He kicked it again, shaking the tree. Henrich backed up and ran shoulder first into the tree and the door opened in front of them with a creak.

"How did you know the door was there?" Cody asked with confusion. "I mean, I didn't know trees have doors."

"Only these trees, my boy." Henrich answered. "Kroger Kid! Come on out! Let's finish this!"

The three stood guard, weapons in hand as the Kid stepped foot from the tree. His hands up in the air, a grin on his face. Not one of a humorous nature.

"This game of yours is finished," Henrich said. "it's over. Return to me my shooter and let us pass."

"I can't let you pass. You'll ruin what they have!"

"That is not your place to decide what happens and what doesn't. The aura is strange and unusual to this place."

"They're seeking to help people. They have faith."

"And it is my duty as a Warslinger of the Heptad to search such places and discover what truly lies within those walls."

"I know. But, they seem happy."

"Seeming happy isn't a sure answer to peace."

The Kid nodded, showing respect with a hint of resistance in his body. Cody gripped the blastshooter as Beth held the handle of the machete tightly. The Kid snapped his fingers.

"There, you have your shooter back."

Henrich reached down and pulled out the shooter, he began searching it for rounds. The Kid held his hand up in a pause.

"Don't fret, Warslinger. I didn't take any of your rounds."

Henrich gazed with a nod, placing the shooter back into

its holster.

"May we now pass?" Henrich asked.

The Kid sighed. "Fair enough."

The Kid waved his hand and the aura presented itself within the forest, however its appearance was greater, and the energy was stronger. Henrich looked up and saw the location of its origin.

"Don't worry, Kid, we won't harm anyone." Henrich said. "Anyone innocent."

"I know you won't, Warslinger. I know your kind."

Henrich signaled for Cody and Beth to leave the forest with him. They walked away as the Kid watched them leave.

"One more thing, Warslinger." The Kid said.

Henrich turned around to face the Kid.

"This isn't our last meeting. We will meet again. Someday."

"That, I am certain of." Henrich replied. "Peaceful nights and blissful days, Kid."

"May you prosper in years." The Kid replied, returning into the tree. The door shut and the tree itself vanished into the light. Leaving an open space in the forest.

The three continued following the aura, until they could hear voices, multiple voices talking to each other and once they exit the forest, they saw the source of the energy. Henrich took a step forward, Cody looked ahead and approached the Warslinger.

"Sir, what is this place?"

"It's a church community." Beth said. "I'm familiar with these places."

"A community, you're right." Henrich said. "But, this one, with the aura, there's something very spiritual happening here."

THE SECRET WORLD

I

The three stood in front of a gated community. Filled with people of diverse appearances and sizes. Cody had never seen the likes of such unification. Beth, on the other hand has, yet, not as it's portraying right before her face. Henrich stared, looking at the people. He found no arguing, no selfish nature, no signs of betrayal. All he saw was love. A love of humans coming together in a world lost to itself.

"This place is incredible." Cody said. "And we haven't even entered it yet."

"Are we even sure we want to go in?" Beth added.

"The source of the aura is coming from this place." Henrich said. "best we find out what it is and continue on our way."

While they stood in awe, the gates opened. Upon their opening, a man approached the three. Dressed in the clothing of a Catholic priest. He was a middle-aged man. He stood facing the Warslinger, gazed him down and up and nodded.

"I see we have new members."

"I wouldn't call us members of your community." Henrich said. "What is this place, truly?"

"Why follow me and I'll explain everything in the form of a tour."

Henrich turned, giving Cody and Beth a look. They nodded as the Warslinger turned back to the priest. He nodded with a hand gesture.

"We will follow."

"Wonderful." The priest said. "By the way, my name is Father Naillain."

"Father?" Henrich said. "There is only one father."

"I know what you're going to say and please, I will explain everything in the tour."

"I will be listening closely."

Naillain nodded. He walked before them as they entered the community and the gates closed soon after.

II

Passing through the gates, they startled and somewhat marveled at the scenery around them. The amount of people staggered Cody, never seeing such since their incident with the Scavengers, however, these seemed more benevolent. Beth respected their hospitality and greetings. Henrich walked beside Naillain.

"How did all of this begin?" Henrich asked.

"Began right around the time the air changed and the Worlds shook."

"I'm aware many places fell. I assume this one right after the worldquake?"

"Yes. I lived not far out of the limits of the city. I saw many of the towers fall upon the streets. Taking away the lives of the scattered. There was nothing I could do but pray."

"And did you receive your answer?"

"I did. But, at the cost of some relatives. They didn't take heed to my warnings of the quake's coming. I told them something was happening across the Worlds. They ignored me. Despised me. Until the day the quake shook."

"How do you know they're gone?"

"I went to their homes. Found them under trees and swallowed by the ground. I knew then, I was on the right path."

"And this path led you here? Being a preacher to those who seek answers?"

"Yes.

They continued to follow Naillain through the community. Seeing gardens, homes, trailers, and facilities. People were living together in what some would call true harmony and prosperity.

"Is there a place here for all these people?" Beth asked.

"Everyone you see here has a roof over their heads and food in their homes." Naillain replied. "No one is of need of anything."

"And you guys grow your own food?" Cody asked. "I saw the cattle over by the gates. Figured they're your meat source."

"Your right. Although, there are some here who live the life of vegetation, no discrimination here."

"I'm not surprised at that." The Warslinger said. "Many sought after food once the tragedies ceased. Vegetation was all that was left in most places."

"We found the cattle trapped in an old farm far from here. We picked them up and brought them here. They breed and bring forth more cattle."

Bleating sounds come from nearby, Henrich turned, seeing a pair of goats passing by. Cody laughed.

"You have goats too?!"

"We do."

Cody went over and petted the passing goats, laughing. They continued walking and stopped in front of the church. A large building with a steeple on top.

"This is where we worship."

"Worship who?" The Warslinger asked.

"The God of the Worlds." Naillain answered. "He's the one who answered my prayers. Gave me this land and brought these people to me. He has a great purpose for my life."

Henrich nodded.

"Good of you to keep in tune with the spiritual."

"It's what we all need in this World."

"I see."

Naillain opened the doors and gestured for his guests to enter.

"After you." Naillain said.

They entered the church, but there was something off in the air. Henrich looked up and the aura was gone. A peculiar nature of such.

III

Inside the church itself were dozens of people. Some were praying, others were fellowshipping, and a few were talking amongst each other. Naillain escorted Henrich, Cody, and Beth inside. Walking down the aisle, greeting the people around them with kind words.

"Everyone seems generous." Henrich said.

"Because they are." Naillain replied. "This is the perfect place for such a harmony."

Upon the greetings, they are brought by Naillain toward a woman, who was tending a family. Naillain stood firm, as did those around him.

"Brandi." Naillain said.

The woman turned around to see him. She smiled and nodded.

"Yes sir?"

"I would like to meet our new guests."

She approached them and extended her hand with a smile on her face.

"Hi. My name is Brandi Bush."

"Beth Grasslands."

"Cody Landon."

"Randolph Henrich."

Brandi looked at him and a quickening came into her spirit. Her smile grew as she looked into the eyes of a Warslinger.

"You're one of them?"

"One of what?" Henrich asked.

"A warrior from the East. The ones who helped in the Battle of Astolat all those years ago?"

"I was involved in that event. It was during my younger years."

Brandi looked at Cody and Beth. Measuring them.

"Now, you." Brandi said to Cody. "You're not from the Western World, are you?"

"Not exactly. I come from the Northern World. It's where I was born."

"I can tell by the way of your speech."

Brandi turned to Beth and turned her head.

"You… you're not from around here either are you?"

"I'm not from any of these places you're all familiar with."

"What does she mean?" Naillain asked the Warslinger.

"She come from another world. Not one of the Four."

"Can't be." Naillain replied. "That would mean…"

"There are other Worlds out there besides our own."

"It goes against our word of law. Our history."

"It doesn't go against them. It confirms them."

"So, where are you from?" Brandi asked.

"I'm from a world called Earth. From a city known as Washington D.C."

"D.C.?" Brandi said. "You have an operating D.C. in your world?"

"Yes."

As they spoke with her, Henrich looked over toward the right of the church and saw an older man, wearing clothing which resembled the Eastern World. Henrich knew there was something peculiar with the man and proceeded to approach him.

IV

The Warslinger approached the older man, greeting him with a handshake. The man stared and hugged Henrich.

"It is time I've gazed upon another." The man said.

"Another what?" Henrich asked.

"One of you. From Old Jerusalem."

Henrich nodded slowly.

"I didn't get your name."

"My name is Abraham."

Cody and Beth approached Henrich and Abraham. The older man greeted them with the same hug he gave the Warslinger. They themselves, weren't sure of what to make of it.

"You're very affectionate." Cody said.

"It's gentle." Beth added. "A sense of love and peace."

"I see you're with the Warslinger."

"We are…" Cody said, looking at Henrich.

"Don't be afraid." Abraham said. "I know of many things. But, if you don't mind, I would like to speak with the Warslinger myself."

"Of course." Beth replied, nodding to Henrich and walking away with Cody.

"Why do you need to speak with me?"

"Because there's a lot to discuss. Follow me."

Henrich followed Abraham to a secure and quiet area. Cody and Beth spoke with others within the church. Abraham brought Henrich to a quiet spot in a corridor of the church and the two sat down in the chairs near a window.

"First off, let me say how it is a true privilege to speak with a Warslinger again."

"Again?"

"I, myself as you can tell, come from the same landmass the Warslingers dwelled."

"Why are you here in Arzareth?"

"I came across the sea sometime after the Fall."

Henrich nodded and sighed. He looked up toward Abraham, seeing the story in his eyes. The words echoing through his ears.

"You were there when it happened."

"I was. Seen everything that transpired."

"You saw the Fall of the city. The end of our tribes and the desolation of our purpose."

"Your purpose was not destroyed. You know this better than the common folk."

"What I know is after the fall, all the Warslingers were scattered. Dispersed across the Four Worlds. I ended up in the desertlands. Traveled through some small towns, came across some peculiar creatures and humans. That trail led me here."

"I can see this isn't the destination. Only a crossroads in your journey."

"It is."

"What are you seeking? Where are you headed?"

"To the Haunted City."

"The Haunted City? Why seek such a place? After all the things you've seen. The blessings you've been given, why go there?"

"Because I need answers."

"You already have that access."

"I've tried. It seems after the fall and our dispersion; everything has gone silent. The City is outside the Four Worlds. It's the perfect place to uncover everything. Why the city fell and why we failed."

Abraham sighed.

"Perhaps, when you reach the City, will you be content with the answers you'll be given?"

"Do I even have a choice."

"You do. You can accept the answers given or decline them and walk away."

"It's a start to a conclusion."

"And yet, how do you intend on reaching the City? The Outer-World at least?"

"There are portals. Gateways throughout the Four Worlds. I intend on finding one and gaining my entry into the City."

"What of the Gate?"

"The Gate of the City will not be a problem for me."

"And this Tubal King?"

The Warslinger stared at Abraham. A knowing.

"How do you know of that name?"

"Because it's an ancient one. Far past the time before you became a Warslinger."

"Then you are aware of his lieutenant?"

"Arkdragon? I am aware."

"How?"

"I lived in the same areas as you did. I was there when you were but a boy and became a man. I am here now, speaking to you as I did my own sons in times past."

"I don't know what to make of all this."

"Make of this in what form?"

"Speaking to you concerning these things. I haven't spoken to anyone in this manner since before the Fall."

Abraham nodded with a smile.

"Then, it is time your journey begins."

Abraham stood up from his seat and Henrich followed.

"I do know what is truly happening here, as do you."

"There's something off about the Priest and this place. The energy around here seems benevolent, but dark."

"You will have those answers soon. But, for right now,

see what you can learn and when the time comes, you will know what to do and I will be there by your side."

The Warslinger agreed with a nod.

"Good. Let's return to the others."

"I wonder what they're all up to?" Henrich wondered.

"Naillain is about to perform an exorcism."

"Exorcism?"

"You will see."

V

Abraham and Henrich returned to the congregation, finding them sitting down upon the pews while Naillain stood at the podium. The Warslinger spotted Landon and Beth, he walked toward them and sat down, Abraham sat behind them as they looked on.

"My family, we have been brought into this tabernacle to cast out a particular spirit from one of our own. Now, I will not point out who this individual is, but as I speak and proclaim the powers of the true god, this spirit will show itself and it will be cast out."

Abraham leaned in toward Henrich.

"You're familiar with all of this, aren't you?"

"I am." The Warslinger replied. "But, in a different way."

Naillain continued, "Now, we have three visitors who have come from the outside and this is the perfect time for them to see what truly dwells in the Four Worlds."

Without a notice, Naillain began yelling out with a loud voice for the spirit to come out and show itself. He screamed it further and continued speaking the phrase. Right after the first minute, a young girl arose from the pews, screaming and shouting from her lungs. Cursing out Naillain, although he continued speaking his words as the spirit moved with the young girl, trying to reach the podium, but was held down by others in the congregation. Cody was sheer afraid, Beth was startled.

"I see you have not budge." Henrich said to Beth.

"I've had my fair share of these things. Frightened me

when I first saw it. Now, I know it's only part of the greater battle."

"What is happening to that girl?!" Cody asked.

"That's not the girl." Henrich said. "What you're seeing is a spirit, a demon who was masquerading and dwelling within the girl."

"And it's upset?"

"Upset for the fact it has to leave her." The Warslinger confirmed. "She is being delivered and set free."

Naillain walked down from the podium and toward the girl. He yelled with a loud voice for the spirit to be cast out and to leave the area. The spirit put up a fight with Naillain and those around him. However, when the spirit caught a glance of Henrich. It froze."

"Come out of her!" Naillain yelled.

The spirit screamed and went silent. The girl fell to the floor. The room was quiet. Yet, above them, the spirit roamed and moved through the air, making its way toward Old Los Angeles, still screaming and enraged. Inside the tabernacle, the girl arose, and the congregation cheered.

"She has been set free!" Naillain cheered.

"Where has the demon gone?" Cody asked.

"It's moving through dry places." Henrich replied. "Seeking rest."

"Will it ever try to return?"

Henrich sighed, looking at Cody.

"They always will."

Sometime later, Henrich remained in the tabernacle with Abraham. The older man could sense something was going on with the Warslinger.

"Why have you chosen to remain in here?"

"The Priest." Henrich said. "Naillain, what god does he speak of?"

"Well, from what I've learned, he believes he serves El, the God of Salvation."

"And does he?"

Abraham shook his head.

"I don't think so. He does serve a god. Only thing is, I haven't been able to discover which one."

Henrich nodded.

"Give it time. It'll reveal itself to us."

"And what will you do when that time comes?" Abraham wondered.

"As I've always done. Finish the work and proclaim El as the true god."

CONVERGENCE

I

Abraham gathered the Warslinger, Cody, and Beth into a room separated from the congregation. Abraham sat them down as he sat in front of them. Looking at the door and taking in a breath.

"What Naillain is about to do may frighten you."

"Frighten us how?" Beth asked.

"He's seeking to convert the three of you into this congregation."

"What's wrong with that?" Cody wondered. "Everyone here seems happy. At peace."

"This place is an illusion." Henrich said. "I noticed it before the gates opened. The aura in the air brought us here. Because the energy isn't a part of the benevolency."

Beth turned to Abraham. A keen look on her face.

"Then, why are you here?"

"Because it is part of a greater plan." Abraham replied. "Far greater than I can speak of."

"And Randolph is a part of this plan?"

"Indeed. He's always known. Yet, he didn't suspect it would bring him to a place like this. Nor meet someone such as myself. Yet, this reality brings people to many peculiar places. To meet peculiar people."

"But, Naillain's way of doing things, appears to be off." Henrich said. "Deeply, I know he means well. Yet, I can only wonder where he received such a message."

"Ask him when he has some time to himself." Abraham replied. "I'm sure he will give you the answer you're hoping."

"I will. Don't worry, I won't cause a disturbance of any kind."

"I know you won't." Abraham smiled. "You're not that kind of man."

II

Naillain stood before his congregation. Speaking on the great things and miracles which have occurred since their fellowship began. Henrich, Cody, and Beth sat in the back of the tabernacle with Abraham.

"The things of which the Worlds have suffered, will no longer matter in the end." Naillain proclaimed. "Because, what's about to come, will shake the foundations of the Four Worlds and they will never be the same."

"He speaks with eloquent words." Henrich uttered.

"You know the types." Abraham replied. "Very talkative."

"Eventually, we will all be caught up together in the Outer-World of Ruachayim and we will remain as one for all eternity."

Naillain looked toward the back of the room, seeing the three visitors. He extended his hand out to them for all the congregation to see. The people turned to glance at the visitors, Cody waved. Beth nodded. Henrich grinned.

"It is with great honor for us to have these three guests in our tabernacle. Fellowshipping with all of us. For they have come from the outside and have seen the tragedies thereof."

Henrich leaned in toward Abraham, keeping his gaze upon Naillain, who's now walking back and forth in front of the congregation.

"The words he's using, I've heard them in such manner before."

"Because he took them from the ancients. Naillain is

only following what he learned while out there in Shemia."

"He's been to the Eastern World?"

"Of course, it explains why he knows much about the spiritual differences and the quickening of the Four Worlds."

The Warslinger sat back. Uneasy feeling within him. Abraham could feel it as well. Cody and Beth were unaware of the circumstances taking place. When Naillain would speak, the energy of his words went out to the congregation. Entering their minds and altering their motives without ease. Henrich waved his hand in front of Cody and Beth.

"What was that for?" Cody asked.

"Protection." Henrich replied.

"Protection from what?"

"You'll soon know."

III

Naillain walked down the aisle of the congregation, making a stop at Henrich, Cody, and Beth. He smiled. They grinned. Abraham sat back and watched.

"I believe it's time you three become official members of this family."

"Wow." Cody said. "Already?"

"I have a general feeling you were destined for a place like this. The Worlds only dream of it."

Naillain extended his and out toward Cody. Cody went for a reach and quickly sat back. Naillain nodded with a stern look. Uncertainty crept upon him. He shook himself and focused on Beth. Speaking to her the same words he spoke to Cody. Beth nodded.

"Do you accept?" Naillain asked.

"This place is special. One of the best places I've come across in this world of yours. But, with all due respect, I must decline. I must return to my world. It's where I belong."

"Naillain stepped back. Nodding slowly.

"That I see." Naillain said. "Much respect to your wishes."

Naillain moved over and stood before the Warslinger. Their eyes locked on one another. Naillain searched Henrich's spirit and was unaware of the Warslinger doing the same. Naillain nodded.

"Do you accept?"

Henrich was silent. He looked over to Cody, Beth, to Abraham, and out toward the congregation. All were awaiting a response from the Warslinger of the Heptad.

"No." Henrich replied. "I do not accept."

The congregation let out a loud gasp and Naillain turned to them, signaling them to be silent. They obeyed their shepherd as he turned back to Henrich. He looked at Cody and Beth. He couldn't understand the true purpose of their decline.

"Why?"

"We're on a mission." Henrich said.

"A mission? It must certainly cannot be higher than what we're doing here."

"It goes forward. Answers must be found for everything that has happened. Everything that has took place across the Four Worlds."

"That a genuine fact?"

"It's a reality."

Naillain nodded. A grin showed upon his face. He pointed toward the Warslinger. While glancing gat the window, seeing its past dark.

"Tomorrow, the two of us shall speak. One-on-one."

"What do you wish to speak on?" Henrich asked.

"Your purpose in the Worlds. My purpose. To see if they are intertwined."

"And if they are?"

"Then, my theory is correct, and the balance is near set."

Naillain turned away and took one step forward. He stopped and turned back to Henrich. He scouted Cody and Beth before focusing on the Warslinger. He could sense something around them.

"There's a barrier around the three of you. Its power is highly strong. I've never come across such a power before."

"Means we're in good company."

"Company with whom?"

"I'll tell you in our talk on the morrow."

Naillain nodded.

"I'm looking forward to it."

The congregation cleared out, leaving on Henrich and Abraham inside. Cody and Beth returned to their rooms.

"What will you tell him?" Abraham asked.

"Everything." Henrich replied.

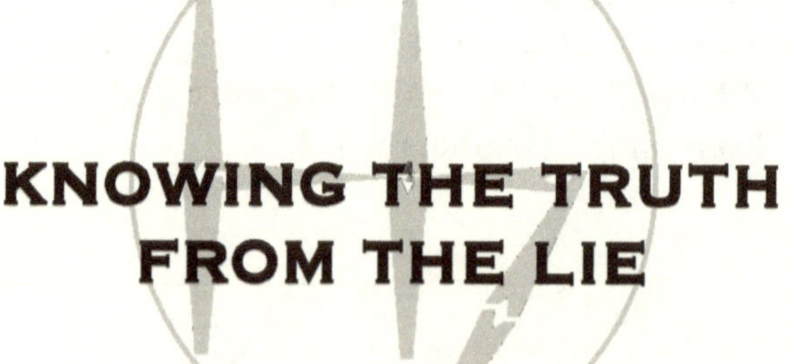

KNOWING THE TRUTH FROM THE LIE

I

A gunshot rattled across the plains, the arkshooter was held still. Holding it was Henrich. His eyes focused, his mind clear. He took another shot across the plains, eventually hitting his target. A scarecrow. Henrich showed a smile of gratitude, placing the shooter back into its holster. He turned around, finding himself standing before his master. Wearing his dark red robe, carrying his sapphire staff. His grey beard gave off a presence of the ancients. A presence of a master.

"Young Randolph, I see you've improved your range."

"Yes, Master Moses. I managed to hit the target this time."

"That I am aware."

Moses escorted Henrich from the plains, toward the small temple. Inside were others, dressed in garb familiar to Henrich's own duster and hat. Some wore leather vests, robes, and diadems. Henrich sat with Moses at the table to eat. Two plates were placed before them by a handmaiden. She was fair to look at. She carried within her a meek and quiet spirit. This pleased Henrich dearly. For there were hardly any in the region which they sat.

"Don't let your eyes wander, boy." Moses said. "For at best, you'll slip and fall."

Henrich caught himself. "Yes sir."

The two ate their bread and meat as another figure approached the table and sat with them. Henrich looked up at the visitor, raising his head from his plate. Seeing another one of his masters. He nodded his head in respect.

"Didn't expect to see me here, did you?"

"No, Master Noah." Henrich said. "I thought you were still in Old Jerusalem."

"I had to come here for duty. It is why yourself and Moses are here as well."

Henrich paused himself, wiping his mouth.

"How's Arthur and Charlton?" Moses asked.

"Being kept occupied with Joshua and Daniel. They've been sent out toward Damascus. Signs of an estranged sphinx were found. Troubling the villagers. They can't sleep nor leave their homes."

"They'll clean out the area." Moses said. "Send the spirit away."

"A sphinx in Damascus?" Young Randolph uttered.

Moses turned toward the young Warslinger. Seeing his enthusiasm in the others' mission. Yet, Moses knew he had to keep him focused.

"You remember why we're here don't you?"

"We're here on a mission?"

"Yes." Moses answered. "Take a look over there."

Henrich looked out in the distance. What he saw was a city. A large one. Standing around the city were three pyramids. One higher and larger than the other.

"What do you see?" Noah asked.

"I see a city of marvelous wonders. I see the pyramids of old. The one our ancestor constructed."

"What else do you see?" Moses asked. "Look closer."

Henrich gazed his eyes closer and what he saw was a shadow looming over the city. The skies above the pyramids seemed clear to the natural eye, but in the spiritual realm, there was a darkness. A malevolent darkness.

"Evil." Henrich said. "I see evil."

Moses nodded.

"That is why we're here in Old Egypt. To uncover what this evil is and destroy it before it spreads further out into the Four Worlds."

"I understand."

"So, is the boy ready?" Noah asked Moses.

Moses turned toward Henrich. He smiled and nodded.

"He's proven himself to me and to El. The boy's ready."

II

Henrich arose from his bed, raising up and looking around the room. Sunlight shining through the windows. Reflecting against his duster and hat. Only seeing Cody and Beth still asleep. He sat up and rested on the side of the bed, reflecting on the dream. He smiled at the memories. His mind warped from the past and to the present, remembering where he is. He stood up and dressed himself. He left the room. Outside waiting was Abraham.

"What are you doing here?" Henrich wondered.

"Figured I would escort you to Naillain's office. He's waiting for you."

"This early in the morning?"

"Indeed. He said he couldn't sleep. His mind was set on the discussion between you two. He has theories and demands answers."

"Demands?"

"I know it sounds forceful. But, they are his wishes."

"And what if he doesn't like the answers I give him?"

Abraham sighed with a gestured expression. He already knew the outcome and the results which would follow.

"Then, he may kick the three of you out or even try to kill you. For being trespassers who seek to do this place harm."

"And what are your thoughts on all of this?"

"I know the truth. When the time comes, I will be standing on the side of justice and victory. Defeat will be on the other end, hoping for a spot."

Henrich nodded with a grin. He extended his hand toward Abraham. He looked down at the Warslinger's hand and instead hugged him.

"Everything is going according to plan."

"We'll see." Henrich said.

Henrich walked down the hall, making a left turn, finding himself facing the office of Naillain. Henrich took a moment and exhaled. He approached the door calmly and as he went to knock, the door opened. As it opened, he saw Naillain sitting at his desk, staring.

"Come on in." Naillain said.

Henrich entered the office and closed the door behind him. The office was silent. Not a sound. The two stared at one another. Naillain stood up from his desk and approached the Warslinger. Looking him down and up.

"It seems the two of us have something to discuss."

"I'm all ears."

Naillain nodded.

"Good. Good." Naillain said. "Let me first begin by acknowledging your rank as a Warslinger of the Heptad."

"So, you're aware?"

"I've been aware before you even approached our gates. You see, I have a keen eye and a traveling spirit."

"Do tell."

Naillain sat at his desk. He gestured toward Henrich to sit and the Warslinger sat down, facing Naillain at his desk.

"You're not the only one here who's had the pleasure of traveling across the Four Worlds. Seeing their wonders and their marks."

"You call it a pleasure?"

"Oh, yes."

"Is seeing the lives of many perishing and suffering considered a pleasure in your field?"

"Depends on who are the perished and suffered. I can only aid those who are like myself. Like-minded and serve the same god."

"You believe you serve *El*?"

"I serve the God of the Worlds. He brought me to this land. This Silicon Valley that once was. He gave me the tools to reconstruct its foundations and in doing so, I have gained a following, a congregation. A family."

"And the exorcism you performed? Was that of your god's power?"

"Yes. Who else can cast demons out of human beings besides him."

"Yet, a foul spirit cannot cast out demons."

Naillain paused. His face became stern. His intent had changed. This is what Henrich was expecting.

"It appears we serve two different gods." Henrich added. "For the God of the Worlds is the ruler of the Malevolency."

"That so?" Naillain questioned. "And where did you learn of this?"

"From my mentors."

"You speak of the originals?"

"They taught me in their ways. It's how I became a Warslinger. A member of the Heptad."

Naillain cocked his head, standing up once more from his desk. Henrich moved and Naillain paused him with caution. No harm. No sense of attack. Henrich understood and kept still. Naillain approached the closet and opened its doors. Upon the opening, Naillain pulled something from the shelves, something large. He turned toward the Warslinger to reveal a weapon. Henrich recognized it well. By its design most importantly.

"Do you know what this is?"

"I do." Henrich replied. "Where did you get it?"

Naillain placed the weapon on the desk, wiping the sheath clean. He removed it, unveiling a sword. The blade was forged in pure gold, the hilt made of carbuncle with a small emerald set in the middle of the hilt and a sapphire placed at the bottom of the handle. The blade itself was thin, with a small thickness in its core. The tip pointed and the sides sharpened. Henrich knew what kind of sword he was looking at and was astonished in his spirit.

"I retrieved this during some excavations over in Old Egypt. I figured someone of your stature would recognize such a weapon."

"It's a *purgesword*."

"Ah." Naillain uttered with a smile. "And what is a purgesword?"

"A blade not from the Worlds. Made for the Seraph."

"This blade belongs to them who are not like us. This explains a lot. The detail. The forging. The stones within. Tell me, how much power do you believe rests inside this sword?"

"Too much for one of our own."

"I don't believe that."

"Doesn't matter what you believe."

"I think it does. I now have the sword. Therefore, I should be able to use it when necessary. For example, I could use it now and kill you. Then kill your two other friends."

"You wouldn't get the opportunity."

"You're willing to test that boast?"

"The test was proven when we first met. I've seen your kind before. Come off benevolent. Seeking friendship, trust, and love. But in reality, you desire control, dominance, and severity."

"I'm not like those you've met before."

"You're all the same." Henrich confirmed. "It's in your nature to repeat the actions of your ancestors."

Naillain slammed the sword onto the desk. His temper grew, yet, he stood back and took in a breath. Relaxing. Henrich kept his eyes focused.

"My congregation cannot see me like this."

"Then, tell them the truth. Tell them what they need to know about you. About this place."

"I will tell them what I choose to." Naillain rebuffed. "They're under my guidance. Not yours. They will do as I say. As I command. In a sense, I am God here.”

Henrich cocked his head. Staring at Naillain, while glancing at the purgesword.

“You know something, ‘Father’ Naillain? You talk of those in the past. Same demeanor and stature. Such like yourself tried to end the Warslingers, to erase them from the Worlds. Yet, I can speak on the opposite. For the Warslingers have always triumphed over their adversaries. For that reason, I can say, the Warslingers will be gathered again. The Heptad will be restored. All will be done at the sound of the last trump.”

“And where did you here this fable?” Naillain questioned. “From one of the books in Old Jerusalem?”

“Moses, my Leader told me.” The Warslinger replied. “Proclaimed it from the mouth of El.”

Naillain took in the words of the Warslinger, he approached the door, opening it. Henrich stood up.

“Best you leave while I get my thoughts together.”

Henrich walked toward the door to exit. After taking one foot forward, Naillain placed his hand on the Warslinger’s shoulder. Holding him steady. The Warslinger was prepared to retaliate, for his left hand was already set upon his shooter.

“Best to tell your friends of our discussion, for I fear neither of you will remain here for long.”

“Is that a threat?” Henrich said.

“Take it however you please.”

Henrich stepped away as Naillain slammed the office door.

III

Henrich walked down the hallway, seeing Abraham, Cody, and Beth waiting for him. From their expression, they knew something was off. By the way Henrich walked toward them, they knew something had happened. Something dark.

"Take it didn't go well." Abraham said.

"It went as we expected." Henrich replied. "We have to warn these people."

"You saw it didn't you?"

"How did he retrieve the sword?"

"He did tell you of his excavation days, did he not?"

"He mentioned it."

Abraham nodded. "We both know the sword doesn't belong to him. Nor to this place."

"It belongs to the Seraph who wielded it."

"What happened?" Beth asked.

"Naillain isn't the man his people believe him to be. He's using them to gain his own purpose."

"That's not good." Cody said.

"He turned the truth into a lie." Henrich said. "That is all I needed to know from him."

"How are we going to warn them?" Beth wondered. "We can't just bombard them with words about their leader going mad."

"There's a way it can be done." Henrich said. "Just give me a little bit of time."

"And what should we do until then?" Cody asked.

"Prepare." Abraham said, nodding to Henrich. "Prepare

56

for what is to come."

Henrich nodded back, walking away from the three and to the outside.

57

IV

Stepping foot on the outside, Henrich saw the congregation. How the people seemed happy and content in their current state. Yet, the Warslinger gazed up toward the sky and above him, he saw what had brought him to this place. The aura had returned and was set over the entire congregation. Over the community landscape. Its energy was dark. It was and is malevolent. As the aura slowly descended onto the people, their faces were shaped and formed differently. The life which was present in their eyes had faded away. The peace from within had vanished.

"Their will is lost." Henrich said to himself. "Their minds erased. Gone."

The people turned their focus toward the Warslinger, who was standing amid them. The congregation began to form a circle around Henrich. He was aware of their motives and their potential goal. He knew Naillain had done this. More than likely praying to the God of the Worlds to send destruction upon Henrich, Cody, and Beth. Slowly, reaching to his shooters, Henrich was prepared to protect himself at all cost. As his hand gripped the handle on the shooter, his head was jolted up toward the heavens. His eyes became clear white. The people stopped in their movement. The Warslinger was frozen still. After several seconds, Henrich regained control of himself. Shaking himself back to steadiness.

"It is time." He uttered, moving with quick pace to find Cody, Beth, and Abraham.

SALVATION OR DAMNATION

I

The Warslinger bolted through the door, startling Cody and Beth. Henrich looked around for Abraham and he wasn't there.

"He went off to find someone." Beth said. "What is going on?"

"We have to leave this place."

"Why?" Cody asked.

"It is not what it seems."

Henrich grabbed the rest of his gear. He commanded Beth and Cody to get their stuff immediately. As they made the moves, the doors shattered. They looked back, seeing the congregation. No longer their peaceful selves. Just energized bodies. No life was set in their eyes.

"What's happened to them?" Beth wondered.

"The aura we followed here returned and fell upon them. Taking away all we once saw."

"Then, where's Father Naillain?" Cody asked.

"He's responsible for this. He's not the man he claimed himself to be."

"Then, let's stop him and save these people."

Henrich shrugged. He knew he wanted to, yet, knew it

wasn't the determined call.

"Can't. we have to leave now."

"Why in a hurry?"

"Death is coming to this place. From the sky, death will rain over this community. All that will be left is the remains of the dead and the rubble of a fevered dream."

Cody looked over to Beth. She turned to him in response.

"He's right." Cody said. "We need to leave."

Beth sighed.

"Look, I know I'm not from around here. But, I need to understand what you mean by death coming from the sky."

"Fire." Henrich proclaimed. "Fire will rain upon this place. Scorching everything and everyone."

"Then, how will we know it's close?"

"Start by watching the animals. Then, watch your steps as you exit this place."

Beth nodded. Henrich nodded back.

"Good. Let's get going."

Meanwhile, Naillain hears the rumblings of thunder in the distance. He rushed over to the window in his office, gazing outside to see dark clouds making their way toward the area. Red lightning flashing within them.

"This cannot be!"

Naillain ran out of his office and toward the cellar. Opening the hatch, he dove in and rushed toward what sat beneath the congregation grounds. A large statue. An idol of the God of the Worlds. A large figure made in gold, standing at near thirteen feet in height with the physique and facial appearance of a man, yet with the wings of an eagle and the eyes of a lion. Naillain bowed before the statue. Paying obeisance.

"I've done all you asked of me. Why is that storm headed here? What is the cause of all this?"

The statue gave off the sudden appearance of smoke. Naillain keened his eyes to get a better look and what was standing in the smoke was a shrouded figure. Cloaked in a black hood and robe.

"It is you." Naillain said with joy. "Please, help me."

"I cannot interfere with such events." The shrouded one spoke. "However, I can give you the source of this circumstance."

"Tell me."

"The visitors. They are the cause."

"The Warslinger and his fellow travelers?"

"They are not the visitors you seek. They desire to destroy all you have built here. Everything. From the buildings, the homes, the livestock, the plants, and even your precious and faithful congregation."

"I cannot let that happen. Tell me what I must do to spare all that I have built under your name?"

"Rid your land of them by any means and the storm will clear."

"And that is all I must do to keep this place protected by your great power and mercy?"

"That shall be all. You have my word."

The shrouded one evaporated with the smoke. Naillain nodded continually, sweating profusely. He wiped the sweat from his forehead and contained himself.

"Rid of them. Yes. I can do that. Yes. I know a way."

Henrich, Cody, and Beth were nearly out of the main building. On a quick turn down a hall, they ran into Abraham and Brandi, who were in a way waiting on them to arrive.

"I was hoping to see you." Henrich said. "We have to go."

"I know."

"You know?"

"I had the vision as well. Same as yours."

"Then you know what's about to happen to this place."

"Indeed. Which is why I must come with you. Brandi and I."

"Why?"

"This path you walk on, it includes the both of us. Trust me, Warslinger."

The Warslinger gave a nod to Brandi. She nodded back. Henrich shook his head, putting on his hat, reaching for his shooters.

"Then we need to get going."

"Yet, you're forgetting something." Abraham gestured.

The Warslinger thought and remembered. He turned toward Cody and Beth, telling them he will return. Abraham kept watch over the group as Henrich returned to Naillain's office. Kicking in the door like it was nothing, he was surprised to find Naillain not inside. Henrich looked around on the desk, it wasn't there. He knew, approaching the closet. He opened the doors and grabbed what he came for.

"You do not belong here." Henrich uttered, putting on the sheath of the purgesword. He walked out of the office, returning to the group with the sword's handle seen over his right shoulder. Abraham nodded with a smile.

"It is coming to pass."

"Let's go." Henrich said.

Reaching the outside of the community, the congregation bolted from all corners. Henrich fired off some shots. He continued firing rounds, until from the ground, black hands and claws came up from the ground. The stench of sulfur engulfed the community. Demons arose.

"Demons!" Brandi yelled.

He paused and reached for the sword. Pulling it from its sheath. The sunlight sparked the golden blade. The congregation and the demons came rushing at him and the Warslinger did what he had to do. Swiping and slashing his way out of the Secret World. Demons clawed against the blade, cutting themselves in the process. Henrich was amazed and continued killing the demons which came toward him in rage. Cody and Beth fired off some shots as well with Abraham and Brandi reaching the community gates.

II

The five make it to the main gate. Yet, the gate is locked and stood strong.

"What are we going to do?" Cody asked.

The Warslinger looked around and from the sky, the thunder roared, and the dark clouds had arrived over the Secret World. Immediately after the thunder, a red lightning bolt came down, striking the church of the community. Setting it ablaze.

"It is happening." Henrich said.

Naillain appeared from the main building, witnessing the church building on fire. Burning down faster at a rate unnatural. The flames had a strange roar to them. As if they themselves were alive and eating the church. Naillain ran toward the front entrance to the church, the doors blew opened by the strong flames, letting out a hollowed screech. Sounds very familiar to a woman's scream in fear.

"No. No. No!" Naillain screamed in anger. "You said you would preserve this place! You gave your word!"

The five watched on, seeing Naillain in a venting rage. Slamming his fists into the dirt.

"What's he going to do?" Beth asked.

"Watch." Abraham said.

Naillain fell to his knees. Nothing left. Nothing to live for. This is what he thought of himself. What had become of his community, he became himself. For if the church was burning, he had to burn with it. In doing so, Naillain arose on his feet and walked into the burning church. Not a thought nor a motion of retreat. Naillain was hopeless. He had nothing else to live for in the Four Worlds. He stepped into the fire. Disappearing into the flames, some of his congregation had caught sight of him and followed along.

"They're killing themselves." Brandi said.

"They chose to die with their leader." Henrich added. "Nothing more."

The rest of the congregation ran amok throughout the community grounds. The sounds of scorching screams echoed from the burning church. Mixed in with the crying howls of the those who remained. Beth looked around and noticed all the animals were gone. Every last one of them.

"They're gone." Beth said. "Just like that."

Henrich felt a peculiar presence of calming in the air. He looked up and made a move on. Abraham also felt it and looked over to the Warslinger. He knew what was to come and turned back to the gate, seeking a way out.

"Then, you know what's about to happen." Henrich said.

A heavy gust of wind came from the east, knocking over the gate, pushing it into the ground, the five ran over the gate remains and stood outside of the grounds. They continued moving further away from the area While doing so, a large whirlwind appeared from the sky and slammed into the grounds directly. Destroying everything and everyone. Due to this, the fire and the whirlwind mixed as one and once the five made it to a stopping point, they saw a flaming whirlwind and people flying into the air, some burning in flames, other not. Cody was astonished, Brandi was in terror, Beth was amazed. Henrich and Abraham paid respect.

"So, everything that was there… the people, the homes… they're all gone?" Beth asked.

"Yes." Abraham said. "Everything. There's nothing left."

"That's a lot of things gone." Cody added. "Just in mere seconds."

Brandi sighed. She approached Abraham and hugged

him.

"Thank you for telling me the truth."

"It was only my duty."

Brandi walked toward Henrich and hugged him as well. He hugged back.

"I'll be willing to tag along. If you'll allow."

"You're on the other end of the grounds." Henrich replied. "You're already with us."

"The whirlwinds are the favorite tools of El." The Warslinger proclaimed. "When the darkness comes and calmness covers the air, it is time."

III

After moving miles away from the ruins of the Secret World, the five continued on their journey. The Warslinger was back to focus on his mission, to reach The Haunted City. During their short travel, they encountered some minor remains from the community grounds. Two brown horses and one dirt-speeder. Cody took the speeder. Abraham and Brandi took one of the horses while Beth took the other. From the wilderness appeared Henrich's horse. The same one from time past.

"Where has that horse been?" Beth questioned.

"He comes when needed." Henrich replied with a smile.

Cody approached Henrich, starring hard at the purgesword.

"I have to ask. What kind of sword is that?"

"It belonged to the Seraph. I guess now, this one belongs to me. Which reminds me."

Henrich pulled the machete from within his duster and handed to Cody. Cody grabbed the machete.

"You're giving it to me?"

"I no longer need it." Henrich said. "Besides, you need something else to wield when in a fight. Something extra."

Cody nodded, looking at the machete.

"I appreciate this."

"Where are we off to, Warslinger?" Abraham asked.

"Back on course. I need to reach the City. I need my questions answered and my fate determined.

They all rode off from the Silicon Valley that once was.

Yet, in the trees, watch on the Kroger Kid. Rubbing his hands together with a grin covering his face.

Later during the day and the travels, Henrich remembered all the mirror had spoken to him. He was sure to believe what it told him, and he would encounter all it said. While traveling, a rushing sound came from above, they stopped and looked to the sky, seeing a large craft flying overhead. With two large wings spanning feet apart. Its body oval-shaped with a circle in the front and back. No windows on either side, only in the front. Glowing neon lights on both its sides and on the wings. The sound it gave off was close to the beat of a humming drum mixed with a horn. With speed that surpasses anything they've met. Cody stood off the bike.

"The hell was that?!"

"A techno-craft." Henrich said. "This far out? Strange."

"You've seen one of those before?" Beth said.

"I have in my travels."

"Then, you know where they're from." Cody said. "We need one, man."

"That's a difficult task." Abraham said.

"How come?"

"Because the location isn't a friendly one." Henrich said. "Yet, it would make our travels from the valleys, ruined cities, and religious communities look like a child's tale. A shepherd's walk across strait pastures in narrow corners."

"What is this place?" Beth asked.

"They call it Mega City. A metropolis built and filled with cybernetic and technological marvels, and, it's where we're headed."

BATTLE FOR ASTOLAT

A CONFLICT OF THE HAUNTED CITY

I

The city of Astolat stood tall amongst its neighboring regions. Astolat is the city of Elaine and her father, Bernard. The city was ravaged by an army. An unseen army, who appeared from the air. The Astolat army combated the strange and ghostly force. The ghostly army overtook the soldiers, killing them within an instant. Bernard took Elaine and they both went into hiding. Having no other choice, but to escape the city as the ghostly army sacked their home and their leader appeared before them. Dressed in a dark violet cloak with his face rarely seen, although his eyes appeared to reveal themselves. The eyes looked dead, but there was another force living through them.

Residing at a secondary home, far into the wilderness, away from Astolat. Elaine writes a letter, detailing the event of Astolat's invasion and sacking by the unknown force. Bernard entered the room, seeing her writing the letter. He's intrigued.

"What are you up to, my daughter?"

"I'm sending word for help."

"Help?"

"Yes. I know of some men who can aid us in taking back

Astolat."

"What kind of me are these that are capable of doing such a matter?"

"A set-apart kind." Elaine said. "They know justice."

She finished writing the letter. Walking outside toward the pigeon cage. Placing the letter, the bird flew in the air with Elaine watching. Bernard approached Elaine from the side, also seeing the pigeon flying away.

"Hope you're right on this cause."

The pigeon flew several miles, until it reached the city of Old Jerusalem. The city was the home base to the Warslingers of the Heptad. The pigeon reached the Temple of the Heptad. Sitting outside the temple was Joshua of Ephraim. The pigeon flew to him, landing in front of him. Joshua sees the rolled letter. He grabbed the letter and the pigeon flies off, returning to Elaine. Joshua entered the temple, seeing the other Warslingers.

"Brothers, this was just delivered to us." Joshua said, handing them the letter.

Moses The Leader grabbed the letter. He opened it and read. The Warslingers stood around him, waiting for him to speak. Moses read the letter to himself and rolled it back up. Nodding, he turned to his brethren.

"It appears we have work to do. First, we make way for Old Camelot. Inform Knight Arthur Pendragon of these details. He must come along with us. For he is also our brother in this walk."

"Moses." Joshua said. "What did the letter inform?"

"It informed of some danger that has been committed. Now, it is our task to rid this malevolency from this place."

The Warslingers make ready to travel to Old Camelot, leaving Old Jerusalem on horseback. In the matter of time, Elaine awaits an answer from the Warslingers as des her father, who worries for Astolat's remains. Believing the ghostly army will turn their city into rubble and ashes.

Entering Old Camelot, Knight Arthur Pendragon was there at the gate to greet his brothers-in-arms. Standing by his sides were Maiden Guinevere and Knight Lancelot. Moses stepped from his horse and walked towards the king of Old Camelot. Extending arms, the two hugged.

"Wasn't expecting to see you this soon." Arthur said.

"Wouldn't be here if it wasn't of importance."

"What's happened?"

"We can talk inside."

"Of course."

Walking inside the castle, they reached the Great Hall, where the Spherical Table sat. the Warslingers all sat at the table while Lancelot guarded the doors. Guinevere left their presence as they started to discuss their matters.

"Now, what's taken place?"

"We've received a letter of distress from the land of Astolat. It appears something has been ongoing in the land for a while and under our sight."

"Invasion from Old Egypt?"

"We won't know until we reach Astolat. We came because we'll need you with us."

Arthur nodded.

"I'll go along. Of course, being a Warslinger myself, it is my duty."

"Believe me, I can see you have plenty to deal with. Ruling a kingdom and being a Warslinger. Only few souls can achieve both titles and become a master at them."

"Speaking of such, how's Old Jerusalem?"

"Peaceful. *El* is there with us. Always."

Arthur nodded with a smile as they headed out of Old Camelot, traveling toward Astolat.

II

Making their entrance in Astolat, the common folk watched in awe and fear as the Warslingers came in on their horses. They made their presence known. Moses turned to Joshua, Daniel, Henrich, and Charlton as they settled their horses near the station.

"The four of you will remain here." Moses commanded. "Keep this place guarded and the people safe."

"Where are you heading?" Charlton asked.

"Myself, Noah, and Arthur will be speaking to King Bernard at their second estate. They refuse to return here until the task is done."

Moses, Noah, and Arthur rode off, leaving the other four Warslingers to settle into the city. They looked toward one another before going separate ways throughout the city, finding a spot and keeping guard. Due to the lack of protection from the Astolatians.

"They carry no weapons." Charlton observed.

"They leave the fighting to the soldiers." Daniel replied. "They don't join in on the battles."

"But, we're supposed to protect them?"

"I know it irks you, Darrain. But, just this once, don't let it bother you."

Far from Astolat, the three Warslingers arrived at the second estate. Seeing two Astolat Knights keeping guard. They approached the door and it opened with Elaine standing in their presence. She ran out and hugged each of them with tears in her eyes. Relieved they received the letter and took the call. Bernard stepped foot outside, seeing the Warslingers. He nodded with great respect.

"It's an honor to have you here, Moses."

"We'll do anything to rid your city of the malevolency which circles it. May we come in and discuss this?"

"Of course."

They entered the home, sitting at the table near the kitchen. Elaine brought them some hot tea, due to the wintry weather occurring. Bernard sat with them while Elaine stood back.

"Tell us what's been happening."

"They appeared out of nowhere." Bernard said. "They showed up and started ransacking the city. Killing some of the people."

"What did they look like?" Arthur asked. "Were they possible adversaries to Old Camelot?"

"No. They didn't seem to be from our world. Nor any of the Worlds."

"You're saying they possessed some mystical power?"

"They must have. To do the things they've done. Levitation, portal binding, teleportation. They had to have been very precise in their arts."

Moses nodded. He looked over to Noah, who also nodded.

'This sounds eerily familiar."

"Do tell." Arthur noted.

"Myself and Noah in the early days dealt with a small army which did such feats. This was when the Heptad was yet to be formed and the Warslingers were few in number. This was during the early stages of the Eastern World War. Those who didn't possess weapons of any kind chose magic as their arsenal. Some we trusted, turned on us, doing the same as Bernard spoke."

"So, will you help us in taking back our city?" Bernard asked.

"I must ask." Noah said. "We just came from your city and only the people are present. No signs of any threats."

"You mean they left?"

"Did they leave after the ambush?"

"Me and Elaine left before we could tell."

Moses stood up from the table. Noah and Arthur followed his movement. A Warslinger custom. Elaine walked to the table and Bernard stood up.

"We will aid you in finding the source of this mystic power. Once it is done, you may return to your city."

"Thank you." Elaine said.

"We're just doing what we must."

The Warslingers exited the home with Bernard behind them. As they sat atop their horses, Bernard approached them.

"You can stay here for the night. We have plenty of room."

"Much thanks is obliged." Moses said. "However, it is best we return to Astolat. To keep guard. We already have four Warslingers present. I will return to you once the job is done."

"I wish you the best." Elaine said.

"Take care of yourselves." Arthur said.

The Warslingers rode off.

Later in Astolat, the four Warslingers have received accommodations in the castle chambers. One to each of them. Henrich sat in his chamber, counting the hours. A knock came from the door, catching the young Warslinger's attention.

"Door's open." Henrich said.

The door opened and Charlton entered. He shut the door behind him and approached Henrich, sitting across from him at the table.

"What is it?" Henrich asked.

"You know me. You know how this all goes. What do you

think's happening here?"

"Some magic wielders probably causing a ruckus. We've dealt with such before."

"Indeed." Charlton nodded. "But, have you ever considered the cost of us doing the work of another? I mean, this King Bernard has knights of his own. Why are we here doing their bidding?"

"I'm not getting what you're speaking."

Charlton sighed.

"We're supposed to protect the ones from evil. Those who can't protect themselves."

"Yes."

"This city already has protection in the form of these knights. We're not needed here. For all *El* knows, we could be needed in Old Egypt or Old Rome."

"I get your point."

"Do you? Because from what I've seen today, you've been blindly obeying every command given."

"I'm not in authority, Charlton." Henrich proclaimed. "Neither are you. We all have our place in the Heptad. In *El*."

"Yes, we do." Charlton nodded in agreement.

He stood up and walked toward the door. Henrich watched him.

"Just remember." Charlton said. "Think about why we're here and not elsewhere. They're something going on and we need to be careful."

"I'll take your word for it." Henrich replied.

Charlton left the room and Henrich laid down on the bed, falling asleep.

Later in the night, Moses, Noah, and Arthur returned to the city and entered their own chambers. All the Warslingers were asleep for the night.

III

The following morning, the Warslingers gathered the Astolatian Knights to the court of the castle. Moses sat before them, giving them instructions on how to prepare for the returning army and the attacks in which will be operated. As Moses continued giving the instructions, a fellow soldier bolted through the doors, his face showing minor scars compared to his damaged armor.

"They're back!" The soldier yelled before falling on the floor.

The soldiers all stood up and ran outside. Moses and the Warslingers held back as the remaining soldiers left the room. Joshua took a step forward, yet stopped by Moses.

"We need to help them."

"And we will." Moses said. "Give it a second."

"A second?"

"This army doesn't know of our presence. Therefore, we have the alterative surprise."

Moses turned to the other Warslingers and nodded.

"You know what to do. Go now."

The Warslingers went their ways outside the castle. Moses walked on and Joshua followed him. Eventually heading outside to see the battle in front of the city and on the castle grounds. They saw the army clearly. Dark armor, scaly and sharp. Their faces covered by their burnt helmets. Moses recognized such a garment.

"This isn't new." Moses said.

"What do you mean, my Leader?" Joshua asked.

"I know who's leading them. And he's close."

The Warslingers appeared from their corners around the castle, catching the army off guard. Henrich and Charlton used their arkshooters, firing rounds in the heads and chests of the mystical soldiers. The rounds from the shooters piercing through their armor like a nail through a leaf. Daniel, Noah, and Arthur swiping through the battlefield. Arthur wielding *Excalibur* while Daniel held the *Faithsword* and Noah carried the *Arkaxe*. The army was quickly being defeated with the Astolat knights cheering on the skills and fighting styles of the Heptad. Through their cheering, Moses and Joshua stepped out into the field as Henrich fired another round at the mystic soldier. The battleground set still with only the cheers of the Astolat knights. The Warslingers came over, standing next to their leader.

"This is not over." Moses uttered.

"Then, where is their leader?" Charlton asked.

"Right there." Henrich said, pointing toward the east, near the entry point of the castle grounds.

Standing before them was indeed a man, covered in scaly armor. Appeared burned, but with a violet and reddish hue. His face was with a helmet, giving him the appearance of having six eyes with a hood and cloak. The Astolat knights attempted to rush him, however, he raised his arms, lifting them off the ground and tossing them across the grounds of Astolat. He was strong in the mystic arts. Moses stepped forward.

"I know him."

"You do?" Arthur said. "How?"

"Because, he was once one of us."

"*Mosheh*." The figure spoke. "We have met once more."

"Yes, we have, Azotus Vorr."

IV

Moses and Azotus stood facing each other. Moses held his staff tightly as the sapphire began to glow.

"It has been some time." Azotus said.

"Not long enough." Moses replied. "You're the leader of this army."

"I am. They came to me after our last encounter."

"Those who sided with you became endowed with mystical abilities?"

"As did I."

Azotus held his arm out and from the thin air appeared a staff. Similar to Moses' own, yet darker, burnt, and glowing wih a violet and reddish hue of energy. The staff was endowed with the same mystical power as Azotus.

"Why don't we settle this like warriors." Azotus said.

"So be it."

The two staves collided, giving off a shockwave of energy. From there, the Warslingers aided the remaining Astolat knights against Azotus' army. The entire area of Astolat was now a battleground with Moses and Azotus standing in the middle, staves colliding and blasting energy. Henrich and Charlton stayed together, firing rounds toward the soldiers.

"What about Moses?" Charlton asked.

"He can take care of himself." Henrich replied. "We need to deal with these soldiers."

The Warslingers take the fight to the soldiers, wiping them out with some of the Astolat knights finishing them off. Moses and Azotus continued their bout, with Moses swiping the staff against Azotus' chest, knocking him across the field. Azotus arose and slammed the ground with his staff, causing a minor tremor. Stumbling Moses.

"Never did like the ground quake." Azotus said.

Azotus rushed toward Moses with staff in hand. In came closer, yet, Moses turned to him with the sapphire staff facing him. Once Azotus was in touching distance, the staff emitted a bright flash of light. The light pushed Azotus from Moses and in doing so, the soldiers of Vorr vanished due to the light.

"What kind of power is this?" Azotus questioned.

"The power you walked away from." Moses replied. "Now, go and never return."

Azotus took steps forward, trying to breach the light's power. But he could not, for the light was far stronger than the mystic power he possessed. The light did come from the staff, but its source was not in the staff nor was it the staff itself. Azotus knew this and vanished before their eyes. The Warslingers looked around and the knights appeared with them. The battle was over. Astolat had won.

Some days later, Bernard and Elaine returned to Astolat and started the reconstruction of the city. Bernard had thanked Moses and the Warslingers for their aid and effort. However, Moses did inform Bernard Azotus would not be returning to his city anymore, but he will return one day to exact payment on the lost battle. Bernard understood the Warslinger's words and chose to assist the Heptad against Vorr once the time arises. Elaine hugged Moses and thanked the Warslingers for their help. They had left the city, returning to Old Jerusalem.

On the path back, Arthur turned to Moses, thinking of Vorr and the battle. He knew the answer to his question and Moses knew it as well.

"Was he who I think he was?" Arthur said.

"He was." Moses replied. "A man once one of us. A Warslinger gone to the malevolency."

CHAPTER ONE

Interstate 5 in Washington state is completely packed. Many are trying to enter Seattle as other drivers try to find their way through. In the front, the drivers notice that a hazard sign has been placed on the interstate for anyone traveling through. No vehicles are moving, just sitting in their current places. One driver, a man, exits his vehicle and proceeds to walk to the front of the interstate. As drivers honk their horns at each other trying to get pass, the man continues walking through.

As he looked closer, he is yanked to the ground. He started to scream as his body is being ripped apart by unseen forces. They bite onto his neck and arms, draining the blood from his body. His screams are heard from the other drivers. As he screamed, other drivers walk out of their vehicles, only to be attacked by the forces as well. Now, the entire interstate is covered with abandoned cars and over a hundred scattered people running for their lives.

The people begin running toward the entrance into downtown Seattle. They continue to run and scream in horror as many of them are being knocked to the ground or yanked behind a vehicle. Many lie on the ground, being ripped apart and bitten in the neck, arms, and thighs. Many are reaching the entrance quickly, but the forces are moving at a faster pace, catching and killing anyone who's in their way.

CHAPTER TWO

In the morning, CNN reports that over one-hundred and fifty casualties were documented in the interstate massacre. Desportan arrived at the public science laboratory in Seattle. Seeing Lucy again, he walked toward her, entering her office.

"Good morning, Lucy."

"Same to you, Doctor."

"So, what's the current situation on the Interstate incident?"

"The bodies have been taken to the morgue. I will contact them in a few about any unusual symptoms to the bodies."

"Very well."

Desportan walked into his office to find an envelope on his desk. He walked over and picked it up. He looked to see who it was from, which was his ex-wife, Eva Desportan. He opened the letter, which was a response about their divorce and what she would receive from it. The letter stated that she demands a BMW be brought to her. He picked up his cell phone and called her.

"Eva, yes it's me. I just received your letter about the car."

"What do you mean 'the car'? it's a BMW that you bought me, and I want it immediately."

"There are more important things going on right now and I can't get to it at this time."

"You better get to it, because there's nothing more important than me receiving my BMW."

"It'll be a while before you receive it."

"Just bring it to me."

CHAPTER THREE

The next day, as Abelard and Lucy were sitting in the office, discussing the bodies in the morgue, Abelard appeared immediately and approached Desportan's office. Desportan and Lucy get up from their chairs and stood up, facing Abelard.

"Excuse me, doctor. I need to deliver an important message here."

"What would that message be? If I may ask?" Desportan said.

"Burn the bodies that are lying in the morgue. They're not safe."

"What do you mean they're not safe?" Lucy said.

"The bite marks on the bodies from the interstate. They're not what they seem to be. An animal did no such thing. You're dealing with a much threatening force."

"What are you talking about, sir?"

"I sense that you wouldn't believe me even if I told you."

Desportan sits at his desk, Lucy sat back down. They allow Abelard to sit in front of the desk.

"Please, tell us."

"What you're dealing with, they're cold-blooded, threatening, terrifying, and bloodthirsty. I'll just tell you that they're vampires."

Desportan turned to Lucy. No word from his mouth.

"Vampires?" Lucy said.

"Yes ma'am. Vampires. I know it seems hard to believe, but I am telling you the truth. Those bodies must be burned immediately. They only have one more night before they fully turn."

"I don't fully understand." Desportan said.

"I am aware of that, doctor. So, what are the two of you going to do about it?"

Desportan turned to Lucy. Not knowing what they could do. He paused and looked at Abelard. He nodded his head.

"Could you tell us more about these vampires, as you call them."

"I sure can."

Abelard pulled out a book from his coat and opened it. He turned from page to page. He stopped at one page and handed the book to Desportan. He put on his reading glasses and looked at the book. Lucy stood up behind him, looking in the book as well. Desportan is confused as to what he's currently reading.

"This cannot be possible to exist." Desportan said.

"They do, sir. They exist among us."

"How did you discover all of this?" Lucy said.

"Because I am a vampire hunter from Germany. I'll tell you more about that later. But, for right now, we must focus on what is here in Seattle."

Desportan read the book and noticed the title *"v12 Virus"*. He looked at Abelard, turning the book around for Abelard to see. Abelard sees it and smiled.

"What the hell is the v12 virus?"

"The v12 virus is what created the vampires of today's time. They appear to be a mixture of certain viruses that are around in vampire folklore. The v5 and Blood Fire viruses. Appears that the v12 virus is the strongest and most contagious virus of the three. Though, it takes time for the virus to fully spread in the human body."

"I've heard of those two viruses." Desportan said. "I'm fully aware of those two."

Eva hung up, which Desportan put the phone down.

"She'll never understand."

Lucy walked into Desportan's office. He looked up and seen her.

"Anything major?"

"The bodies at the morgue. They all have bites marks on their throats, arms, and legs."

"Bite marks?"

"The coroner's not sure as to what caused those bites."

In the Museum of History and Industry, a man is currently walking through. He is German doctor, a fellow historian and he's also a vampire hunter. He is known as Professor Abelard Ekkehardt. Abelard scans the aisle for anything related to vampirism or any source that connects to vampires. As he approaches the final set of aisles on that row, he finds a book related to vampirism. He sits at a table in a corner as he scans through the book quickly. He stopped at one page, which showed an illustration of a horde of vampires.

Abelard squinted his eyes at the pack and thought back about the interstate incident. Abelard knows that vampires are the cause of the interstate disaster. Abelard left the museum.

Abelard arrived at the hospital which has the bodies of the deceased in their morgue. He walked toward the receptionist's desk.

"Excuse me, I would like to speak with your coroner, please."

"I'm not sure if I can allow something like that."

"Please, madam. It is of a serious matter. The bodies are not safe to be examined on."

The receptionist cautiously pointed to the direction of the

morgue. Abelard looked and thanked her. He moved quickly through the amount of people in the hallways. He turned two corners before reaching a door that says "Morgue" on its nameplate.

"Finally."

Abelard walked into the morgue and seen firsthand the amount of bodies lying inside. He spotted the bite marks.

"Dear God."

The door opened behind him and it is the coroner. Abelard walked up to him and pointed at the bodies.

"What are you doing in here, sir?"

"Please, you must listen to me. You need to rid of these bodies and burn them immediately! They're not safe to be around."

"Why don't I just call security to see if you're alright."

"I am alright! I've been doing this job for over thirty years. I know when a body should not be messed with and you're trailing on some thin ice here, young man."

Abelard walked to the door, before exiting the morgue, he turned to the coroner with a concerned look on his face.

"Please, burn the bodies. All of them."

Abelard walked out of the morgue and exited the hospital. The coroner walked out to see if Abelard left. As he stood at the door, a doctor passed by, looking the same direction.

"What was the problem?"

"Just some crazy old man, that's all."

After the moon set, a group of vampires, some with hair, others bald. All of them are pale and have clear eyes and razor-sharp teeth. Others have some sort of ooze coming from their mouths. Over a dozen of them gather at Crown Hill Cemetery. The dozen vampires move quickly to a grave site. The grave dug opened. The vampires sit or stand in an orderly fashion. They seem to be waiting for something or someone.

A few begin to hear someone walking over to them. A tall force, wearing all black with black hair and pale eyes. He even has a pair of sharp teeth of his own with sharp nails. He stood above the dozen vampires as they bowed before him. The tall force raised his arms.

"My children. I am Dunkan, The Dark One. Your lord and master."

The vampires cheer at Dunkan. Praising him as their God.

"I have gathered you all here on this night to pass down a message of The Fated Ones. We shall transform this city into our homeland. The interstate was just the beginning as we much kill as many as we can. Whether they are man, woman, or child, we must make a stand here and claim it as our own. Once we claim this city, we will travel south to claim more. After a few months, we'll have this entire country and within a year, we'll have the whole world at our disposal."

The vampires cheer with sounds of snarls and growls. Dunkan smiled down at them, loving the attention he was receiving.

"We must fully take command and give praise to The Fated Ones. For if not for them, I would not be standing in front of you today to give you this message. We must stand tall and we must conquer all!"

All the vampires growl in praise. Dunkan walked away, looking back one time with a huge smile on his face.

Inside an office of a home sat a man, in his mid-thirties with black hair wearing slacks and a buttoned-down shirt. He is Dr. Allan Desportan, a scientist who works on different species of animals and sometimes works on finding cures for diseases. As he sat at his desk, examining a file that contained information about Polio, he looked up at the TV in his office, he noticed it was CNN and they were broadcasting the instate event, Desportan leaned in and realized the running people were heading downtown in Seattle. As he watched the live footage, he seen the forces that were chasing and killing the people. Deep pale skin, some with red eyes, glowing from the reflections of light, others with clear eyes and long fanged teeth coming from their mouths.

Desportan stood up from his desk and goes for his white lab-style coat and someone is knocking on his door. He walked to the door and opened it. A Caucasian woman with long wavy black hair. She wore a buttoned-down shirt with blue jeans and looked to be in her late twenties.

"Dr. Seward." Desportan said. "What are you doing here?"

"I came to check to see if you just saw the footage of the interstate."

"I did." I was about to drive near it to examine the creatures."

"I think you shouldn't go." Seward said. "Its best that you stay indoors to avoid this. I'm sure we'll be involved with this tomorrow."

"You have a point there." Desportan said. "Thanks for warning me, Lucy."

"You're my colleague." Lucy said. "I have no choice but to watch out for you."

Lucy left Desportan's home. He walked back inside and sat in his office, still watching the live feed of the interstate. Now, there are not many people running on the streets, they're just lying on the ground either dead or dying.

"What in God's name is going on."

MORE WILL BE REVEALED IN THE UPCOMING
VAMPIRE NOVEL TITLED...

THE

<u>HORDE</u>

2021

GLOSSARY

This is a short glossary of words, meanings, beasts, weapons, vehicles, and locations revealed so far across The Haunted City Saga through The Legendary Warslinger and Redemption of the Lost

Adamah: The name of the World as a whole. Combining all four worlds. Named after the first human to walk upon the world.

Arkshooter: The revolver pistol shooter wielded by the Warslingers of the Heptad. Made from the gold and wood as the Ark of the Covenant.

Arzareth: The Western World. Also known as the Western sector of Adamah.

Benevolency: The true good of the Worlds. A bringing force of peace, love, and hope.

Blastshooter: A shotgun hybrid of the shooter.

Bull-Lion: The mutated beast with the body of a bull and the legs and tail of a lion.

Choiros: The mutated furry hog with large tusks from its mouth. Its size is of a small beetle vehicle.

Demons: The spiritual creatures who roam the Four Worlds due to the Malevolency.

Dire Scorpions: Large sharpened insectoids. Significantly larger than the traditional scorpions from Shemia and Khamain.

Dirt-Speeder: The primary source for fast travel across the landscapes of the Western and Southern Worlds.

Ghouls: Spiritual entities which roamed throughout the Valley of Death.

Ghosts: Spiritual entities of the previous life. Capable of traveling across worlds and dimensions.

Green Man: A plant/human hybrid. Its body covered in foliage, oak leaves, and small branches. Its face is covered with a beard made of grass.

Heptad: The significant title of the primary Warslingers. Meaning "seven".

Hevoc: A small semi-deserted town. Known for its encounter with Randolph Henrich.

Horse-Spider: The mutated beast with the body of a horse and the legs of a spider.

Khamain: The Southern World. Also known as the Southern sector of Adamah.

Lamia: The demonic creature which takes the appearance of a young girl. When in true form, it appears reptilian in nature.

Land of the Survivors: The land occupied by Wade and the Scavengers.

Leprechaun: The dwarfed species which lives across the Western and Northern Worlds. Usually sighted by the presence and scent of gold.

Maarab: The West Sea.

Malevolency: The true evil of the Worlds. Capable of corrupting all life. Whether material or spiritual.

Minotaur: The hybrid man/bull beast whom resides in the labyrinth of the Dark Forest.

Mount of Divination: The mountain of which Randolph Henrich defeated the Mercenary Man and received a glimpse into the future from the Mirror of Fate.

Old Camelot: The ancient city of Camelot. Led by Knight Arthur Pendragon, a Warslinger and King of Camelot. It was taken siege by Morgana Pendragon during the Fall of Old Jerusalem.

Old Egypt: The remains of Ancient Egypt. The land hasn't changed since the ancient periods.

Old Jerusalem: The ancient city of Jerusalem. Still intact from its ancient days. The dwelling place of the Warslingers of the Heptad.

Old Los Angeles: The remains of what was Los Angeles, California. Only several buildings remain standing after the events of the War of the West.

Phantom Dog: The supernatural beasts that surrounds death. It's red eyes are always remembered. Seen by Randolph Henrich in *The Legendary Warslinger*.

Purgesword: An ancient sword made from the fires of the Seraph. Lost during the Fall of Old Jerusalem, later taken by the Secret World, later retrieved and carried by Randolph Henrich.

Qedem: The East Sea.

Qeramah: The ice wall surrounding Tehomayim and the Four Worlds.

Red Demons: Stronger Demons. Malevolent entities with the scent of sulfur. They primarily roam in packs. Smaller in nature and much faster in speed.

Revolver Shooter: The standard shooter in the Worlds.

Ruachayim: The Outer-World. Also regarded as the spiritual realm outside of Adamah.

Salamanders: Elemental creatures of fire known as the *"Nature Spirits"*.

Sapphire Staff: The legendary staff carried by Moses The Leader.

Savel: A town reminiscent of pilgrimage and full of secret sodomy.

Sea of Tabbur: The center-ocean between the Four Worlds.

Shadowic Creatures: Supernatural creatures whom dwell in the shadows and have enhanced abilities connected to the darkness.

Shemia: The Eastern World. Also known as the Eastern sector of Adamah.

Shroudoks: Shadow insects that reside wherever there's little light present.

Sphinx: The estranged creature mentioned by Noah in Damascus. Its appearance is half-man (head), half-lion(body), and half-eagle(wings).

Strander: A fellow traveler. Usually from a foreign location.

Succubus: The feminine sexual creatures that feed on the energy of Man.

Techno-Craft: Large and quick skycrafts made in Mega City.

Tehomayim: The Full Ocean which surrounds the Four Worlds.

Teman: The South Sea.

The Dark Forest: The supernatural wilderness set at the end of the Valley of Death.

The Haunted City: The titular city. The location where Randolph Henrich searches for truth concerning the universe.

Tsaphon: The North Sea.

Valley of Death: The desolate land covered as a desert.

Vrylolakas: Druid-Like Vampires. Some fought against Randolph Henrich in *The Legendary Warslinger*.

Warslinger: A holy knight and warrior. Usually born and trained in Old Jerusalem. Servants of El, enhanced with spiritual abilities given to them for their cause.

Wolf-Hawk: The mutated beast with the body of a wolf with the wings of a hawk and talons of an eagle.

Worldquake: A large, great tremor that can cause massive damage to structures and landmasses.

Yaphean: The Northern World. Also known as the Northern sector of Adamah.

ABOUT THE AUTHOR

Ty'Ron W. C. Robinson II is the author of several works of fiction. Including the *Dark Titan Universe Saga* series (*Dark Titan Knights, The Resistance Protocol, Tales of the Scattered, Tales of the Numinous, Day of Octagon*) and *The Haunted City Saga* series. Also of other books (*Lost in Shadows, Hod, The Book of The Elect, Symbolum Venatores, etc.*) and One-Shot short stories More information pertaining to the author and stories can be found at darktitanentertainment.com.

Twitter: @TyronRobinsonII
Instagram: @tyronrobinsonii

Twitter: @DarkTitan_
Instagram: @darktitanentertainment